SHADOW
THE COUGAR OF FLAT CREEK

written by Jean Craighead George

illustrations by John D. Dawson

introduction by Jane Goodall

With many thanks to...

Margot Snowdon, Gillman and Marge Ordway, Louise & Ralph Haberfeld, Sophie Craighead, Judy Pigott, Connie Kemmerer, Emily Knobloch, Sunny Spiedel, Rita Smith, Hazel Lynn Singer, Erika and Anthony Stevens, Emily Novak, Laurie Wilson, Connie Wieneke, Laura Ladd, Kris Gridley, Katie Nelson, Nancy Nordhoff, Ariana Snowdon, Greer Terry Freed, Nell Fuqua, Nassim Assefi, Cory Curtis & David Adams, Maria Clark, Julie Butler, Lori Bowdler, Teresa Meadows, Patti Boyd, Toni Farmer, Chelcie Jonke, Robin Moyer, Nancy Resor, Amy Staehr, Jeanie Staehr, Pamela Stockton, Karen Terra, and ALL the magnificent women of The Book Group. And to all our individual contributors and the following foundations and organizations:

The Hill-Snowdon Foundation · Community Foundation of Jackson Hole · Seattle Office of Arts & Cultural Affairs · National Endowment for the Arts · The Cougar Fund

Thank you to Jean Craighead George's three children — Twig, Craig, and Luke — for permission to complete this beautiful book that Jean started and never got to hold in her hands.

For the beauty contained in this book, special thanks to artists John Dawson and Tracy Lamb.

Above all, thanks to Lisa Rullman Craighead & Charlie Craighead for working so hard on behalf of this book, and the legacy you now hold in your hands.

To you all, our most heartfelt thanks and gratitude.

252 East Pearl, PO Box 13275, Jackson WY 83002
www.whitpress.org 206-295-1670

Shadow, The Cougar of Flat Creek
© 2018 Estate of Jean Craighead George
Illustrations by John Dawson © 2018
Design by Tracy Lamb of Laughing Lamb Design, Jackson, Wyoming

ISBN: 978-0-9836983-4-0

Library of Congress Control Number: 2017960339

First Edition: 2018

INTRODUCTION - JANE GOODALL

I've written before about my memory of a children's book that I read when I was nine years old. I had found it in a secondhand bookstore, and it was about the friendship between a boy and a wild cougar. Reading it was one of those childhood encounters that gently nudged me further toward a life of conservation. That cougar was everything a child could want in a wild animal friend. I've looked numerous times for the book, hoping to see if my memory of it is accurate, but it's never reappeared.

But now we have a new book to inspire children. And it, too, is about a wild cougar. Only this time there is no warm relationship with a kind human. This time, it reflects the reality of life for wild cougars in North America — misunderstood, hunted, trapped, and feared by humans. But still beautiful and fierce in their own world.

Jean Craighead George had a long career writing stories from her own experiences. In this book she wanted to tell about the life of a wild cougar, but she had never seen one. She talked to our mutual friend Tom Mangelsen, and he told her about wild cougars that are drawn to the edges of town by herds of deer being fed by well-meaning residents. The cougars hunt at night, and are feared this close to people's homes. Before long, they are trapped or killed. This was the story Jean needed – a cougar learning that a human is not its friend.

The lesson Jean makes is that for humans and wild cougars to coexist we need to leave them alone. The one thing they need most is space – wild country where they can hunt, hide, and play their part in the natural world.

I hope this book inspires its readers to help give cougars their wild space and protection from hunting. That's all they need from us.

—Jane Goodall

Whit
Press

Jackson Hole, Wyoming • Seattle, Washington • www.WhitPress.org

SHADOW

THE COUGAR OF FLAT CREEK

It was twilight.

Shadow, a young female cougar, quietly strode to the entrance of her birth cave on a wooded butte above Flat Creek.

She looked across the valley to the mountains.

Her mother was somewhere out there. But Shadow was not looking for her or even for her brother. She was looking to the wind, the pines and aspens, the wild flowers and hidden animals. It was time to find her own territory.

She slipped down the butte side in the waning light. The spots of her kittenhood were gone and her now tawny fur blended into the sand-colored outcrops.

She came to the bottom of the butte. A badger was foraging for mice and ground squirrels. Shadow ignored him and slipped out into the valley.

At a stream she stopped and pressed her sensitive ears forward. A blue grouse fanned his wings in the twilight. She ignored him.

Shadow was two years old now and leaving her mother's homeland forever. There would soon be new kittens for her mother to tend. Shadow must go.

Cautiously she raised her head and tasted the wind — WOLVES!

Shadow slipped through the sagebrush as ephemeral as wind-blown dust. She came to an old twisted cottonwood tree. She climbed it.

Lying flat on a sturdy limb she looked down on the gathering wolves. Shadow had learned from her mother that wolves can't climb trees. She felt safe. The wolves glanced up at her and trotted off.

She leaped down and took off again in search of a home. Slinking through moonlight she came to a wetland around a beaver pond. She quenched her thirst. Suddenly a bull moose was in the pond dribbling water-plants from his huge mouth.

She backed off. He could kill her with a strike of his hooves. She could kill him with a grip of her jaws. She chose not to. The moose chose not to. Both turned and ran.

Shadow came to a grassy meadow. A herd of elk were grazing among the blue lupines and green grasses.

She purred.

Elk were excellent food. Her mother had often led her to a brush-covered carcass of one she had hidden for Shadow and her brother.

13

Elk had been Shadow's favorite food. Without thinking she stalked them silently. Creeping on her belly, she went through the tall grasses.

She trembled a grass blade. An elk saw it move and burst into flight. A little cottonwood tree that the elk was about to eat was saved. It would now grow tall and its roots would help stop the bank of the stream from eroding.

A mallard fluttered in the pond grasses. Shadow snapped, caught it, and ate for the first time that day.

Shadow rolled in the grasses and then rested near the cottonwood sapling and purred. She liked this land, its meadow and mountain forests. Deer, elk and moose lived here. Could it be her new home?

She crawled under the gnarled roots of an old pine tree to sleep for the day and blended with the shadows. A man hiking a trail through the meadow near her did not know she was there. He thought she was only a shadow.

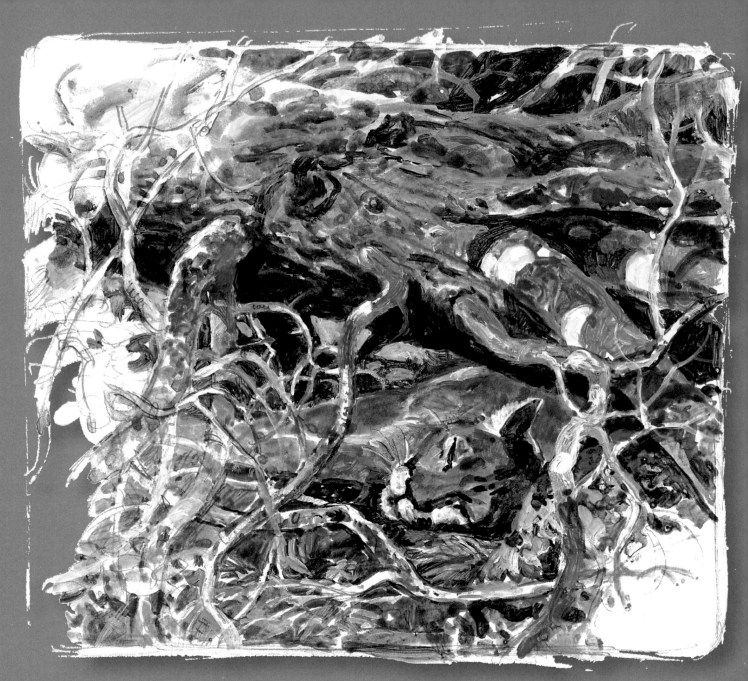

At noon Shadow awoke to see a truck moving on the far side of the meadow. It stopped. Tar, the hunter, and his dog, Gunner, got out. Shadow ran up into a pine tree. They came across the meadow. In Tar's arms was a gun.

Suddenly Gunner smelled Shadow, barked and ran to the old pine tree. He howled beneath it.

BOOM! Something whistled past Shadow's head. She leaped to the ground and vanished like a ghost into the sagebrush. Tar and Gunner did not see her go.

Out in the Osagebrush Shadow took a zigzag route as she stepped on stones and logs to lose her scent. When she came to a river bottom, she vanished into the shadows and fading daylight. At sun-up she found a large rock outcrop. It was the color of her fur. She lay down on it to sleep. No one saw her but a bluebird catching insects.

That evening Shadow was awakened by a young cougar. He was hissing at her. She preferred to be alone, even from her own kind. She got up and walked off. But something smelled tasty. Curiously she looked back. The young cougar was holding a ham bone he had stolen in his jaws. The ham smelled delicious.

The young male lay down and finished his treat then set off to get more. Shadow sensed his mission. She followed him. They traveled to the edge of a paved road. Across it were houses — and garbage. The cats crossed it and crept to the edge of a back yard.

"There he is," shouted Tar. A shot rang out.

The young cougar leapt in the air and fell dead. He lay on the cold ground — the tragic end to a short life. The young cougar's mother had been shot when he was six months old. From that moment on he had to hunt for himself. He did not do well for lack of a teaching mother. He managed only to kill rabbits and mice. He had turned to eating garbage.

"There's another cat!" Tar shouted and pointed to Shadow. She slipped into the tall grass. He raised his gun.

He saw no cougar — only ravens flying away and screaming, light and shadows moving beneath them.

ow Shadow knew that men carry guns that can kill. She turned away from the ham bones, the back yard and the hunter. Gunner howled and ran after her.

She eluded him by jumping over an animal that the wolves had killed. This strong scent threw Gunner off her trail as he followed the scent of the wolves. Shadow wove through an aspen grove and slid under a rock overhang. She lay still listening to Gunner foolishly following the wolves' trail up a mountain instead of her.

At dark she stretched and leaped from the rocky
overhang. She glided miles down the valley, but she
was not safe. Elegant houses were scattered around
her. They smelled of "man." She moved on.

At dawn she stopped in the willows beside a
mountain footpath far from her mother's
territory. She fell asleep in a willow thicket.

The next night Shadow came to the valley
that her father had once called his home
— a hundred square miles of meadows, willows
and waterfalls. Now no cougars lived here.
There were just tree stumps and houses. She
sought the cover of the sagebrush and glided
on in the dark.

Coming over a ridge she startled a grizzly bear in a huckleberry patch. He rose to his hind feet and snarled at her. She drifted away like smoke. Not even the bushes trembled she moved so smoothly. Wiser now, she stayed in the safety of the high mountain fir forest, sleeping by day in caves or on cliff tops.

Near a mountain stream Shadow made a kill. It was enough meat for a week. She would stay nearby until she had eaten it all.

But a woodsman came upon the carcass and recognized the tooth and claw marks on it as a cougar kill.

He telephoned the famous cougar-killing man,
Tar, to come get her. Tar drove miles
to the woodsman's cabin.

That afternoon Shadow heard Gunner
baying and ran to her kill to save it.
She wanted that food.

Standing over it she smelled Tar and his gun.
She grabbed a hind-quarter and ran with it.

Gunner was howling along her trail. He was getting closer. Shadow dropped the food and leaped into a fir tree. Gunner stopped at the hind-quarter and began to eat.

Then Tar arrived. "Where's that ghost cat?" he shouted to the dog and kicked him.

But Shadow was gone. She had slipped out of the tree and was running along fallen logs and jumping over brooks. In this manner she ran deep into the forest, eluding Gunner and Tar. Cougars can't run for long distances, so when she felt safe she rested, then ran again.

She stopped hours later
in a forest wilderness.

No roads led into it.

No houses spoiled it.
No hunter prowled here.

31

A sign
on a tree
read:

"No Hunting"

Shadow
had found a
new home.

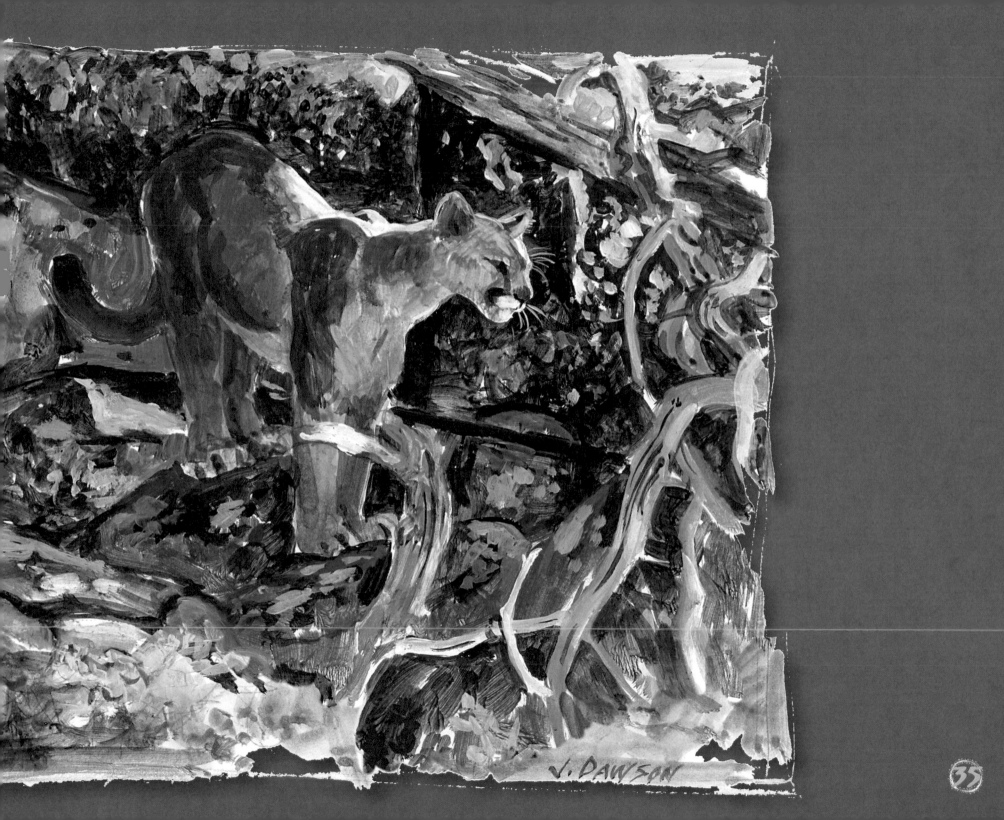

J. DAWSON

ABOUT THE AUTHOR

Jean Craighead George finished writing the children's book, *Shadow - The Cougar of Flat Creek*, shortly before her unexpected death. She wrote it to educate children about this majestic apex animal.

Jean Craighead George wrote more than 100 books and won the 1973 Newbery Medal for *Julie of the Wolves*. She was instrumental in connecting children with wildlife and to the out-of-doors through her enchanting story telling. *My Side of the Mountain* won a Newbery Honor Award in 1960.

One of the best children's authors of our time, Jean's work continues to leave a mark on the hearts of innumerable children who devour her books.

"*Shadow - The Cougar of Flat Creek* was the last book that my mother, Jean Craighead George, worked on. Her nephew Charlie came to visit her and edit a final draft. She was her usual completely focused self as she worked on the text, taking breaks for hamburgers at the diner or hot dogs at the food truck in Croton. They finished the draft and Charlie left for Wyoming. Four days later she died. She used to say she wanted to die "over the letter K," working to the end, she did. She would be delighted that this book turned out so beautifully and her voice carries on."

— Twig George,
Cockeysville, Maryland

Aunt Jean...

I **was so lucky** to grow up with Jean Craighead George as my aunt. Every book she wrote turned into an adventure and she pulled all of us around her into the endless stories she created.

The Craighead family has a pattern of threes; Aunt Jean had twin brothers, Frank and John, and all three of them had three children each, making nine cousins in the bigger family. As far back as I can remember our families shared each other's lives; we were like a big pack of coyotes. Jean included us in her storytelling adventures with raccoons and owls and crows, and my father, Frank, and his brother John brought Jean's family to the West to see their research on grizzly bears and golden eagles and ravens. And we all had wild animals in our lives – stories within stories within stories.

Jean was a master at finding a narrative where the rest of us just found interesting animals or a beautiful landscape. She had a unique writer's sense – a hole in a tree or an animal track in snow opened her eyes to some natural saga. When she looked at the eastern hardwood forests of New York she saw a perfect place to run away and live off the land (*My Side of the Mountain*). When she observed wolves in arctic Alaska she saw the connection between wolf packs and the native Iñupiaq people (*Julie of the Wolves*). In so many ways, and wherever she went, Jean was tuned to the wild drama around her.

Jean loved the wide-open spaces of arctic tundra and western prairie. She loved swamps and everything that crawled or swam in them. She loved plants, and bugs, and she loved people. She loved both New York City, New York, and Cooke City, Montana. She loved the creatures she found in her back yard and the most elusive animals of the world.

So when Jean heard about the work of her friend Tom Mangelsen and his efforts to protect wild cougars, she thought about this creature she had never seen despite all her travels in cougar country. Why had she never seen one? Certainly they had seen her — she'd hiked enough trails in cougar habitat. She realized the importance of a safe and untrammeled habitat for the cougar's survival, and she saw a story from the cat's perspective. How and where does it hide? How does the world look from its hiding places? What dangers does it face?

Jean thought about it off and on for two years, asking questions and reading about cougar encounters. I was visiting her in New York one October and she asked, "What could I do for the cougars?" She was ninety-one years old at the time.

Half joking, I said, "Write a book for them."

The next morning she got up at 5:00 a.m. as usual, sat down at her computer, and it all came together in her head. She began to type. By the time I awoke and made a cup of tea she had written the first draft of this book. She changed a few words later, and named the cat Shadow, but everything else came to her that beautiful morning in Chappaqua, New York. "*Shadow – The Cougar of Flat Creek*" is 100% Jean Craighead George inspiration.

— Charlie Craighead
Moose, Wyoming

ABOUT THE ARTIST

John D. Dawson was born and raised in San Diego, California. From the age of three, John and his family knew that art was his calling. With the complete support of his working-class parents, they allowed him to follow his dreams.

He has illustrated for the National Geographic Society, National Park Service, United Nations, Audubon Society, and many other notables. Over eleven years John worked with the United States Postal Service creating the 'Nature in America' series. It is one of his proudest accomplishments.

More information about and examples of his work can be found at jdawsonillustration.com.

SKETCH BOOK

39

Northern flicher - common
Red-shafted

Columbian Ground Squirrel

41

SUPPORT FOR THE INDEPENDENT VOICE

- Whit Press is a nonprofit publishing organization dedicated to the transformational power of the written word.

- Whit Press exists as an oasis to nurture and promote the rich diversity of literary work from women writers, writers from ethnic and social minorities, young writers, and first-time authors.

- We also create books that use literature as a tool in support of other nonprofit organizations working toward environmental and social justice.

- We are dedicated to producing beautiful books that combine outstanding literary content with design excellence.

- Whit Press brings you the best of fiction, creative nonfiction, and poetry from diverse literary voices who do not have easy access to quality publication.

- We publish stories of creative discovery, cultural insight, human experience, spiritual exploration, and more.

WHIT PRESS AND THE ENVIRONMENT

Whit Press is a member of the Green Press Initiative. We are committed to eliminating the use of paper produced with endangered forest fiber.

Please visit our web site for our other titles.

www.whitpress.org

Colophon

The first commercially successful typewriter was invented in 1868 by Americans Christopher Latham Sholes, Frank Haven Hall, Carlos Glidden and Samuel W. Soule in Milwaukee, Wisconsin.

Our title type and all of the body copy is set in ITC American Typewriter. This font was designed by Joel Kaden and Tony Stan in 1974. It is an ode to the afore mentioned invention that shaped reading habits and the idea of legibility. The type was designed as a compromise between the rigidity of its ancestor and the expectations of the digital age, ITC American Typewriter retains the typical typewriter alphabet forms, lending the font a hint of nostalgia.

The interior stock of our book is 80# white opaque smooth made by Finch Paper LLC of Glen Falls, NY. The jacket wrap is 100# Titan gloss C2s with a matte layflat lamination.

Book design by Tracy Lamb of Laughing Lamb Design, Jackson Hole, Wyoming. All illustrations are by John D. Dawson © 2018.

Print production by Bookmobile Craft Digital
5120 Cedar Lake Road, Minneapolis, MN 55416